TO ME, HE IS LOVE

VARNAA VARUN

To Varun,
The love of my life, my biggest supporter, and my greatest inspiration.
For always believing in me, even when I doubted myself.
For standing by me through every joy, every struggle, and every moment in between.
This book is for you, for us, and for the love we've built over the years.

Contents

Foreword

Love stories are not always perfect and its all about understanding and trust and even the small and unspoken bond between two hearts.
To Me , He is Love is not just my story , it's a heartfelt journey of emotions, patience and love that grew over time.
When I met Varun for the first tym I found a spark at him but I never imagined he would become the most beautiful part of my life.
This book is the reflection of those moments that made my heart race.
Through this pages, I invite you to enjoy our journey and to believe in magic of love.
Welcome to the world of Varnaa Varun

With warm regards
Varnaa

Preface

Writing To Me, He is Love was a journey in itself—one that brought back countless memories, emotions, and the essence of what love truly means to me. When I first thought of putting our story into words, I hesitated. But Varun, the person who has always encouraged me to dream bigger, to write without fear, and to believe in the beauty of our journey, stood beside me through it all.

This book is not just a collection of memories but a testament to the years we have spent growing, loving, and understanding each other. It's a celebration of our past and a promise of all the chapters yet to come.

I thank him, for his unwavering faith in me.
And I thank God, for writing our story long before I put it into words.

Acknowledgements

Writing this book has been as emotional journy and it wouldnt been possible without the love, support of my special person

First and foremost , I would thank varun, the love of my life and my greatest motivation and the reason behind this book exist.

His presence in my life is a blessing and I love the way he stand beside me with love, warmth and memories we have built together.

I also want to thank my parents for shaping me into the person I am today.

Special thanks to the universe for bringing varun into my life and for guiding me through every challenge with love and warmth.

    With love and gratitude

VARNAA

Prologue

Love stories often begin with a moment—an unexpected glance, a fleeting connection, or a feeling that sneaks into the heart before one even realizes it. Mine began the same way. When I first saw him, he was just another face in the crowd, someone I barely noticed. But as time unfolded, he became the only face I longed to see.

This book is not just a love story; it is the journey of us. A journey of two souls who unknowingly drifted toward each other, faced moments of uncertainty, and yet, found their way back every time. It's about the silent glances, the unspoken emotions, the misunderstandings that tested us, and the love that kept us together.

Varun, my love, my strength, and my unwavering support, has not only been the reason for this story but also the one who encouraged me to write it. There were days I doubted myself, unsure if our journey was worth telling. But he reminded me that love, in its truest form, deserves to be remembered. And so, I wrote.

To Me, He is Love is not just a reflection of the past; it's a continuation of our story—the next chapter of our lives. As you turn these pages, I hope you feel the depth of our journey, the emotions woven into every word, and above all, the love that made it all worth writing.

I thank him, for being my love and my muse.
And I thank God, for writing our fate before I ever held a pen.

— Varnaa

1
The love of My Life

"Love has a remarkable way of revealing itself in unexpected moments".
Sometimes it's loud and obvious; other times, it's a quiet whisper, gently finding its way into our hearts.

Every glance, every look, every word, every moments and every coincidence might seem significant, yet they can shape something far greater than we can imagine.

When we look back, we can see the puzzle pieces falling into place, leading us to something beautiful and unforgettable.

Love has a wonderful way of revealing itself in the most surprising moments! Sometimes it's loud and clear, while other times it feels like a gentle whisper, gradually finding a home in our hearts.

1.1 A Silent Admiration

Love has an interesting way of sneaking into one's heart when one least expects it. To me, it happened in the beautiful corridors of Presidency college, to which I'd joined as a psychology student.

Coming from a girls' only school then stepping into this co-ed institution was exciting yet overwhelming. I was shy, unsure, and completely unprepared for an emotional hurricane that would soon hit my heart.

When I first saw him, he was merely a face in the crowd-our class representative, serious, and always on the move like a restless leopard. But one fine day, while he was standing before the class making an announcement, I found his eyes meeting mine for two fleeting seconds. At that very second, something inexplicable had stirred within me, like I had a glimpse of the trailer of my future. From that day on, I found myself, more out of will, seeking for him with my heart skipping a beat every time we crossed each other's path.

But fate kept pulling us closer and closer without any of us intending to do so. There were three incidents that finally forced every one of them-the third incident into a different way of bringing me closer to him.

The Number one Incident

On a day, he approached me and asked for my phone number. My heart started racing. Panic and anger flowed into me-Why is this boy asking my number? He is my classmate, still an unknown for me. Without hesitation, I bashed him and turned away by getting anxious6. Then later, I came to know that he needed it for a class WhatsApp group. Oh, how foolish I had been! Now, I just laugh at the memory of my overreaction.

The Attendance War

In college, the Tamil class was conducted in the Physics department as a combined class with physics and psy students. The professor often assigned the task of marking attendance to the class representative or to the girls sitting in the front row. I used to take attendance quite often and did it very seriously; absent students were marked absent, especially boys who deliberately missed classes because our professor bored them with his off-topic lectures. The ever dedicated class representative, however, did just the opposite of me. Everyone is marked present, including the left one. This infuriated me. How could he do something like that? Unable to contain myself, I confronted him and brought it up with him, thinking he was abusing his authority.

The truth came out later and shocked me. Most of my classmates came from financially struggling backgrounds, as was common for a government college. Most did part-time work to pay for their education, and not attending classes meant they would be paying fines for attendance shortage. He marked them present, not through negligence, but he did it so that they did not incur monetary losses.

Tamil class? It didn't bother to be important for the total attendance percentage. I had assumed an awful lot erroneously about him.

The Lost Photo Incident

Once again, he was responsible for collecting our details, basic things like passport-size photos, as well as contact numbers. Days later, I got to know that he had lost my photograph. As soon as I heard it, my blood boiled. What if someone used it illegally? My heart pumped fast with anger and fear-I was vigilant and always cautious with boys in college. In my annoyance, I vented all of it on him, showering him with very bitter words.

His responses, however, stunned me. Innocently, he told me he had left the papers in his pants and washed them without knowing it with his clothes. I just stood there dumbfounded. Not careless-just genuinely forgetful. For the first time, a new kind of feeling started pouring into me. I was not just angry anymore but had a new feeling that was quite different-regret: had I been too harsh? That was when I actually realized how innocent he was and softened toward him in a way I had never expected.

Love That Withstood the Test of Time

First, it was a kind of irritation and misunderstanding that slowly transformed into admiration and something flung much more deeply. It has now been eight full years since I first saw him back in June 2017, yet even today, no matter what, each time I see him, my heart skips. Those eyes that look at me, every moment shared, even by chance, every moment shared-in only deepening my feelings toward him.

But that was just the beginning. Days kept bringing fate in unexpected places, drawing lives closer together, encasing therein more and more laughter and confusion and a growing bond that neither could deny.

What Happened Next?

After knowing his true self, my perception of him altered slowly. He has not become less than just a classmate, or just someone who annoys. There is depth and kindness here, with an unarticulated sense of duty. But did he see me in the same perspective? Isn't there more fate had in store for us?

Unexpected incidents happened every now and then as college life went on, and the most heartfelt conversations went on gradually filling the gaps between us. Those times made me blush, some made me think of what I really felt, and some made me want that time would stay.

Our love story was still unravelling, and little did I know, the best was yet to unfold.

1.2 A Support System

It was much more than asking for notes and sitting in classrooms. It was all about making friends and creating moments that brought much closeness into everyone's lives, especially life at college.

In our college, the students organized functions like Freshers' Day and Farewells for the junior and senior classes. He was the class representative convenor responsible for organizing these programs.

Most of the students came and just enjoyed such events. But he worked very hard on coordinating the students, collecting funds, planning budgets, and being more confined without anyone's help. Nor did he ask for help, nor did he complain.

He took all the work and did it by himself: though such works are supposed to be done jointly with others, he takes it on himself.

Just like every other afternoon after classes had ended and most students had gone home (since it was 8 AM-1 PM for arts and science colleges to run usually), he was still there sitting in the classroom, wholly involved in his work-in that he was struggling to count the money he had collected for the Freshers' function and was somewhat lost in balancing out the budget.

I paused for a moment, watching him. An untouched lunch box lay next to him; he hadn't eaten. I knew he took food from home and travelled close to two hours each way, either by train or bus, to attend college. Yet here he was eating lunch, all alone working and expecting no one to give him a hand.

Something stirred within me. Without much thought, I asked him, "Do you need help? Should I assist you ?"

He looked up, surprised.

Perhaps he had not expected to find me there, much less an offer of assistance. Our eyes met for a second or two, and then, thankfully, he nodded. "Okay," he says kindly, allowing me to sit beside him.

And just like that, we worked together to collect money, making a budget to organize the function.

This was our first time together, even though he was my classmate.

There were no meaningless words, no forced conversation, just the quiet understanding of two people working towards the same goal. However, deep within me, I knew that it was something more than that, something precious as well as memorable to hold. I had just stepped into his world, not as just another classmate but as someone who noticed his efforts and wanted to be there for him and to support him.

This Afternoon Will Ever Be Remembered in Silence

That was a memorable afternoon. As we both concentrated on the work, stealing glances at his serious face, moving fingers in counting, the determination in his eyes caught my vision. He was known among people to do everything in favour of everyone without any hesitation, yet none of them had even minded their question over asking, "Are you fine?"

I had taken my first steps to being that person without realizing it. I didn't know, but one thing was for sure- something is good the future brings. And I was excited to see where we would go from here.

1.3: A Union That Goes Beyond Words

One afternoon, surprisingly, He asked me to help him, the man who doesn't expect anything from anyone related to work or personally ask me a favour..! It was not a dramatic change, nor would it be noticeable to anyone else. But I feel it inside me.

I have always been good at managing things right from my school days. All class responsibilities were given to me by teachers—not so that they'd feel nice about me, but because I just loved and respected them. That carried over to college as if it had to, and naturally, we found ourselves working together more often.

It started just as an innocent offer to help with budgeting events but soon blossomed into a different, more profound relationship. Later, we acted like co-workers in handling many works relating to classes, things tied to departments, and organizing and planning; there were also collections and submissions of assignments, putting attendance other office-related formalities, and even applications for scholarships. Everything worked, as We were good at dividing the work well.

The Unpaid Understanding -

Once in a while, on some days, we sat with quiet concentration, just listing down seminar topics, totalling marks in papers, entering marks, and calculating attendance percentages. There was no need for either of us to speak. We had an understanding that it was without saying that made it so easy to work together.

Though the conversation stayed mostly austere between us, there was something uniquely uplifting about our shared moments. I wanted those moments because I relished doing the work and enjoyed his companionship. The way he concentrated on his work, undertook responsibilities without even a tiny word of complaint and carried the class burdens on his shoulders all made me admire him more.

Above all, he had started noticing me.

Was I just another helper to him? I wasn't only doing work for that fantastic sense of responsibility but because he unknowingly pulled me close to him.

I have no idea and would be spared a minute to wait and see.

The Bond Deepens

Days became months, and with time, we kept getting closer. To others, it looked like two responsible people working hand in hand, but in my mind, everything we were doing together fell far beyond that. Each moment spent, every silent glance through a stack of papers, every unspoken agreement of how to divide the tasks-everything meant something to me.

Call it good luck, but everyone in our department has some idea about us. With the work we did, we were trusted with responsibilities by professors. In addition, classmates could rely upon us for guidance and help. We didn't just work for our department; we worked for our classmates, who are obviously friends, no one left, and our professors. And we enjoyed the work that made us happy.

But there was something that would distinguish him as something more than just a responsible class representative.

He was not a guy who was just focused on his studies and tasks; he was looking for something more meaningful-that was to make the class feel like a family.

His Efforts to Keep Us Together

As a class representative, he ensured all 40 of us were close during our three-year journey. He arranged for everyone to put their names in the birthday plan for 3 years, collected money from everyone, got surprise cakes, and ensured no one felt left out.

He did it hard not because he had to but wanted to. He wanted our class to be more than just a batch of students but wanted to be able to consider us family, having this great UG batch that remains interconnected even after college.

That kind of thing made me admire him again because he was not just a good class rep- he had a heart that genuinely cared for people.

Unknowingly, he attracted me more to him with every little thing he did.

Shared Responsibility

One of the things that connected us was our habit of cleaning our classroom. We stayed back after all had left to collect all the waste paper, turn off the electricity, and ensure all windows and doors were closed correctly. We don't talk about it, but it has become an unspoken routine done by just the two of us.

It wasn't really about cleanliness. It was sharing responsibility, an understanding that this class was our space and that to both of us, this was something to be cared for in the same way.

Little did I know, however, that day would come in the future, bringing moments when my feelings would deepen and deeper...

1.4 The Growth of Respect

As time passed, my admiration for him grew more deeply, quietly, subtly, yet undeniably strong.

I am sure it wasn't the kind of admiration that stemmed from infatuation or physical attraction at that age. It was something more profound, something that felt like an artist admiring a masterpiece or a musician getting lost in the rhythm of a song.

I noticed the little things about him—"the rhythmic sound of his shoes against the floor, the unique blend of oil and sweat on his face after a long, exhausting journey, and even the familiar scent of his perfume that reached the classroom before he did".

These small details became part of my everyday life, and I slowly realised it; I started searching for him more.

Waiting for Him

Being a hosteller, I often reached college early, but rarely lately.

I used to collect the classroom keys from the peon and open the doors, ensuring everything was in place before the day started. But soon, it wasn't just about opening the classroom—I found myself wandering around, waiting for him to arrive. Every day, I wait for him at the place where I have opened.

It felt almost ironic. I lived barely ten minutes away from college, yet I would patiently wait for the one who travelled two hours every day—rushing between trains and buses, pushing through the morning crowd, to make it on time for the first-hour department period.

Sometimes, I called him to check if he had reached the college gate. Other times, I found myself unconsciously helping him in small ways, like delaying the professor from taking attendance by asking questions or making delays in collecting the attendance from the class tutor to give him those extra few minutes to arrive without being marked absent.

His Endless Hustle

There were days when I felt sorry for him.

He always hurried to catch the train, submit forms, take Xerox copies of class notes, and run to fulfil responsibilities. His shirt would often be drenched in sweat, his hair and beard soaked with the heat and dust of travel, yet his eyes burned with a relentless fire.

He never complained, never let his exhaustion show.

Instead, he carried on with his responsibilities with a sense of quiet dedication, and I found he made peace even in his endless responsibilities.

Perhaps in these moments, I admired him the most—not just as my class representative, but as a person who never backed down and let hardship define him.

Little did he know that amid all his rushing, someone was watching him, silently caring for him, and falling for him a little more each day...

1.5: The Inner Struggle

With the calendar pages turning from day to month and one departmental function after the other coming and going, classes resumed. In all these works, we collaborated well, keeping our partnership only professional. I was much in his vicinity, occupying the seat next to him, organizing events, sharing responsibilities, etc. But through it all, I consciously attempted to remind myself not to fall for him.

I did not know what love was; I had never seen it outside the unconditional love of my parents and my sister. I had never had a crush or very temporary flings or puppy infatuations. Love was something far away. I had never thought of it for myself.

And so I fought it. I stayed away from him deliberately—not looking at him, passing him by without acknowledgement, and sometimes willfully being indifferent or borderline rude. I told myself these strange feelings would pass if I created enough distance. My heart would return to its former calm, untouched status.

But Life Had Other Plans...

Whenever I tried to shove him away, my thoughts dragged him nearer. The more I tried to ignore him, the more my thoughts were filled with him. Not that he tried to impress his presence in dramatic or overwhelming ways, but subtly—over there in the corner, like a soft melody persistently refusing to dissipate into silence.

And he, being so calm and composed and indifferent, never questioned my distance and never tried to bring a change in my behaviour, which only made him ever so more attractive as he quietly crumbled the walls I was desperately trying to build. Unknowingly, he ravaged the doors of my heart and shoved an empty chair there—almost as if saying he would stay as if he was meant to be there all along...

I had no opportunity to defend myself anymore. Love had entered my heart and was not going anywhere this time.

1.6: The Quiet Pull

No matter how much I tried to suppress it, I felt myself being pulled toward him in ways I couldn't fully understand.

Other than going to college and attending the classes and doing the work that was given to me by our professors, I didn't have any bond with any of my classmates, as they seemed so unconnected to me; I talked only if there was any necessity or if they need any help. But I had always been more attached to my hostel friends than my college mates. They were my world, the ones who filled my time college time; perhaps that's why I instinctively avoided him when I saw him in the corridors. Even as my heart ached to turn back for just one more glance, my feet carried me forward as if he were just another stranger.

Actually its not my intension ignore him, I feared the reaction of those around me. Few of my hostel friends, (not everyone) had a habit of teasing, spinning harmless yet relentless jokes about anyone they thought I was making friends with, especially boys. I didn't want to be the subject of their playful interrogations. Rather, they had lots of fun moments at a later period, and did I want them to read too much into something I was still figuring out? So, I ? kept my distance.

But he noticed everything.

When I was absent for even a day or two, he was the one who asked about it. Even my benchmates wouldn't bother, but he did. I thought that he was the class rep.

It was never grand just a simple question, a glance of concern—but that was enough. In a classroom of forty students, his attention found me, and that realization sent ripples through my heart.

I told myself it was just friendship, that he was fulfilling his duty as a class rep. Yet deep down, I knew that wasn't true. The way he noticed my absence, his eyes searched for me, and I instinctively sought him out in classrooms and corridors—none of it was ordinary.

I was afraid to admit it, but something was changing. Something had already changed.

1.7: The Space Between Us

Beyond our shared responsibilities, department work, and long hours spent together breaking heads to find solutions, he belonged to everyone. He had an effortless way of being there for people—not just as a class rep, but as a listener, a good friend, a special friend who knows anyone's secret admirer than mine. He never judged, rushed to give advice, or made it a big thing. He listened, offering his quiet presence as comfort.

And people gravitated toward him.

Both boys and girls found it easy to talk to him, but the girls especially sought his company—those who needed someone to listen without offering a solution. I watched him spend time with them, laughing, joking, and existing in a space that wasn't tied to responsibility.

Two or three girls in particular—good-looking, confident, playful—seemed drawn to him. And he, in turn, welcomed their presence. They would gather around him, teasing, laughing, sharing inside jokes, and even feeding them food. I wasn't a part of it. It wasn't as though he deliberately chose them over others, but I could see that they enjoyed his company, and perhaps, he enjoyed theirs too.

He had a small gang—a mix of our classmates, a few seniors, and some girls—who went out after college, spending time together, unwinding in ways I never had. I would hear their laughter here and there.

And? I remained where I was, on the other side of an invisible line.

This may be why I hesitated so much to connect with him. Perhaps this was why I sometimes avoided him, even when my heart longed to see him. It was a strange mix of emotions—an attraction I didn't want to acknowledge, a fear of crossing boundaries, and a silent effort to protect myself from feelings I wasn't ready to face.

I told myself that I had no right to feel anything. Even as a friend, I had never tried to cross that boundary. We were coworkers and teammates; if he saw me as anything more, he never said it. Even when he noticed my absence and asked about me, I wondered if it was just his nature—to be kind and responsible.

So, I did what I knew best.

I distanced myself, not physically, but emotionally. I spoke to him only when necessary, only when it was about department work. I kept my expressions neutral, my tone firm. I never showed a smile and never let my emotions slip through. No matter what I felt inside, I made sure that, on the outside, I was just a classmate, a coworker—nothing more.

And then, I found something else from someone at some point.

He had a girlfriend.

He never spoke about her openly, but I learned that during free hours, especially language hours, we would be allowed to use mobile phones, and he would spend time talking to her.

And in that moment, my heart whispered something I wasn't ready to hear.

"How lucky she must be..."

To live in those eyes. Sitting beside him, not touching, just existing in his presence.

I didn't know who she was. Maybe she was beautiful; perhaps she was the kind of girl who had caught his attention the way he had unknowingly captured mine.

I didn't want to admit it, but maybe—just maybe—I was jealous.

Not because she was his but because she was someone he had chosen.

1.8: A Heartfelt Gift

Days passed. Before I knew it, his birthday had arrived the next day—February 21, 2018. Everyone in class planned to celebrate him, showering him with gifts and a cake-cutting moment of joy. Friends surrounded him, all eager to make his day special.

But where should I stand?

I wasn't his friend; I wasn't part of his gang and never bothered. At most, I was just a classmate, a co-worker in department duties. But still, I wanted to give him something. I wanted to make a small memory of his day, even if I didn't know how.

This was the first time in my life that I was buying a gift for a boy. I had no idea what to get. It wasn't like I could ask anyone for advice without raising questions.

That evening, the day before his birthday, I went to a stationery shop with my friend, not intentionally buying him a gift but giving her company. That's when I saw them—tiny miniature erasers. Something about them drew me in. I bought two:

One was a shoe—because I had unknowingly fallen for the sound of his footsteps, the way he carried himself in his shoes.

The other was a gun—a random thought crossed my mind that boys liked cars, bikes, swords, and guns. Now, looking back, I laugh at myself—why did I buy a gun miniature for a boy so gentle, who never liked violence?

I didn't write anything fancy, just a simple "Happy Birthday, Rep Anna." That could be my way of hiding my feelings, of keeping the distance intact.

That day, he was sitting with his usual group—his so-called gang, who were always around him. I hesitated but eventually called him aside to give the gift. He came to me with a Galaxy chocolate in his hand.

He asked everyone in the class about their favourite chocolates and bought them for each person. So, I wasn't unique. I was just one among many. "10 in 11," I thought to myself.

Still, I was happy inside. At least, we exchanged something for that moment—a small, quiet memory between us.

That afternoon, I returned to the hostel with mixed emotions. I was happy I had gifted and received something from him in return. But deep down, there was a heaviness in my heart.

I hadn't been there with him for the celebration or stood beside him when he cut the cake.

That day, I made a silent wish—to be there with him on his next birthday and make it more memorable.

1.9 : Let's Start with Friendship

So far, I have written about how I wished to celebrate his next birthday, so what happened next?

It was our second year here, and we started speaking and becoming involved in department activities there. And it was a time the NAAC committee visited our college for ranking,

We, the Department of Psychology, plan to start a counselling room called Vanavil. We 5, which became a core team to work on as the head of the department trusted us more next to the other professors; that five core team included him and me

I was thrilled that it must be a long process to be with him and spend more time with him apart from class work as a representative (I am not but him). Those moments will be cherished when we start working after college hours. Even during college hours, our head prioritised us to complete the work first and scheduled the important classes based on our convenience; that time, we made colourful vanavil, where he and I started to talk a lot rather than simply working like a robot. Creativity speaks.

We started to share ideas and make it happen; he helped me cut the shape for that huge vanavil model and even helped me paint it. I found he was happy doing those works, unlike other boys.

I loved his patience and dedication towards the work, and our team's effort made it happen; on that time, I found 3 of the others took a rest in between and relaxed, but we two worked without any tiredness, as we enjoyed working it. Finally, I found a person like me who enjoys liking the job and whatever we are doing.

We both made that program hall and place clean by washing the floor and dusting the benches without hesitation; despite the other boys in our class, he seemed unique and enjoyed the little things he did.

After that program, I started to speak to him like a friend rather than a classmate or coworker who worked like a robot; we began to share more, like discussing what to do, what not to do and how to do and make the program successful.

It's not about how we did it; it's about how we made it; even at that age, we made mistakes and learnt from our flaws.

I found something unique and happy while being with him and started to explore more about him and express myself to him.

Let's see what happens next...

1.10: A Spoonful of Kindness

Time moved forward, and I stepped into my second year of UG, but something inside me remained stuck. A conflict with my best friend in the hostel had left me completely alone. She had been my constant—my only friend, my companion in everything from eating to sleeping to studying. But after a small argument, she left, unwilling to find a solution.

I cried in silence, holding the weight of loneliness for more than two months. No one was around besides me. The emptiness felt hard, yet life moved on. Classes continued as usual, assignments piled up, and I went through the moments like a ghost, present in body but lost in mind.

One afternoon, after class ended at 1 PM, I had some work to do before returning to the hostel. Walking past the canteen, I saw him sitting with his so-called gang—laughing, eating, and living in the moment. I hesitated momentarily, but he noticed me before I could turn away. With his usual warmth, he invited me to join them.

I sat beside him, and for the first time in a long while, I felt something I had forgotten—calm.

Amidst the chatter, something unexpected happened.

He took a spoonful of lemon rice and brought it near my mouth to feed me.

I was surprised by his gesture.

Did he do that? With a little hesitation, I took a bite. It wasn't about the food—the warmth, the kindness, the unspoken understanding in that small act.

"Thank you," I said softly. "I actually hadn't eaten."

He just smiled as if it was the most natural thing in the world. Later, I would learn that he had this habit—feeding the people around him first before eating himself. How sweet he is.

That moment broke something inside me. The walls I had unknowingly built around myself began to crack. I started talking—not just about random things but about me. My family, my parents, their health... stuff I had never told anyone in college, let alone him. Words poured out before I could stop them.

And then, somewhere between sentences, I paused.

Why was I saying all this to him?

He wasn't my best friend. He wasn't someone I had ever shared my struggles with before. And yet, somehow, sitting beside him, I felt safe enough to open up.

And maybe that meant something.

1.11: A Gesture of Support

In my department, the professors were always friendly and encouraging. Knowing that I was good at painting, one of my professors approached me with an opportunity—a drawing competition focused on awareness about suicide prevention, addiction, and mental health. Alongside the competition, a walkathon was organized under the Happiness Chain program.

The rules for the painting competition were simple: we had to complete our artwork at home and bring it for exhibition. The walkathon was scheduled at Besant Nagar Beach early, at 5 AM.

I started working on my painting the night before the event. However, there was one problem—I had no idea what an A3 sheet looked like. I searched in my hostel, asked around, and even Googled it, but nothing gave me a clear idea. Frustrated, I finally called him.

Surprisingly, he didn't know either. But instead of dismissing my concern, he immediately came up with a solution.

"Just stick two chart papers together like a poster and paint on it," he suggested.

It made sense, so I did precisely that.

As soon as I started painting, I became deeply involved in it.

Hours passed. After almost five hours of standing and painting, my hands ached, my back felt pain, and exhaustion slowly crept in. But I wasn't even close to finishing.

It was getting late—almost bedtime—and my energy was draining. Hopelessness took over. I stared at my unfinished painting, feeling helpless. There was no one around to motivate me. And so, I called him again.

I didn't expect much—just someone to hear me out. But he listened patiently when he picked up, understanding precisely what I was going through.

"You've been standing for almost six hours, right? Of course, you're exhausted. But don't give up now. You've come so far."

He didn't just tell me to keep going; he stayed on the call, talking to me until I finished the painting.

He shared stories from his school days, making me laugh and distracting me from the pain and fatigue I had at that time. Slowly, the exhaustion faded, and before I even realized it, the painting was complete.

I let out a sigh of relief and smiled.

"Finally done!" I said, feeling lighter than before.

"See? I knew you'd do it," he responded with a warmth that made my heart feel at ease.

Grateful beyond words, I thanked him. As a gesture of appreciation, I invited him to see my exhibition at the beach the following day. But he already had plans with his family—it was a Sunday.

Though a little disappointed, I understood.

The next day, I woke up early and caught an auto headed to Besant Nagar Beach for the competition. I set up my painting, confidently explaining its message to the visitors.

To my surprise, some of my classmates and seniors had also come to participate in the walkathon—something I hadn't expected.

Then, something even more unexpected happened.

I won first place.

After a long time, I tasted victory. It wasn't just about winning—it was about achieving something I had poured my heart and soul into.

And I wished he was there to see it.

Despite the joy of winning and celebrating with my classmates and seniors, I longed for him. I badly wanted him to be part of my happiness.

So, as soon as I got the chance, I called him.

"Guess what? we won first prize!" I exclaimed, my voice filled with excitement.

He sounded just as happy as I was.

"That's amazing! I knew you could do it!" this was the exact dialogue he said, and at that moment, I felt satisfied.

Even if he wasn't physically there, his presence in my journey meant everything.

1.12: A Step Forward

Slowly, I started talking to him more, sharing moments of my life, including the painful breakdown with my best friend. He never offered advice or tried to fix things, but he listened—truly listened; that's what he was expert.

His silence wasn't empty; it carried warmth, a quiet reassurance that he was there for me.

Our occasional calls became more frequent.

At first, I had reasons for discussing during exams and clarifying department work, but deep down; I knew I was finding excuses to hear his voice.

And maybe he felt the same way.

After the painting competition, something changed. Some of his friends—classmates I had never spoken to—became my friends, too.

That victory didn't just bring me a cash prize; it opened doors I hadn't considered. And most importantly, it connected me to him in ways I never expected.

I started returning to the hostel late, even after college hours, talking with him and my new friends, the so-called gang. But time was never on my side. He had a part-time job then and would leave soon after classes, cutting short the moments I cherished. I found it harder and harder to say goodbye. Some days, I even held back tears as I watched him walk away. No one noticed—not even him.

Yet, no matter how brief our time together was, he never left without ensuring I had eaten. It had become a habit, his small yet thoughtful gesture of feeding me before he went off to work.

On some days when I stayed back, I spent time with our new group. Other times, I would leave with him, walking together to the bus stop. I did it because I miss him. But no matter where I was, my emotions remained hidden and unspoken. Even he had no idea what was growing in my heart.

Step by step, I was becoming a part of his world. And the more I did, the harder it became to imagine myself without him.

1.13: A Shoulder to Lean On

After the intense moments from the past few days, we barely had time to breathe before another challenge arrived, but it was unforgettable.

Our department function was approaching, and our HOD had assigned us various responsibilities to ensure its success.

However, at the same time, we had another significant commitment to participating in an exhibition where we were to put up stalls for a competition based on the field of psychology.

While the department function was necessary, the exhibition felt like an exciting opportunity that genuinely mattered to us. But our HOD had other plans. She decided our priority should be the department function and wanted us to focus entirely on it, disregarding the competition.

Despite our enthusiasm for the exhibition, most of my teammates, including him, were burdened with responsibilities for the department function. Unlike them, I was the only one who somehow escaped the workload and dedicated myself to preparing for the exhibition. I had no time constraints and an open space for ideas. Balancing everything independently was challenging, but I was determined to put in my best effort. Though my teammates, including him, couldn't contribute much initially, they still supported me whenever possible.

When the department function finally ended, we had just one day left to prepare and arrange the stalls for the competition. That day, everyone gave their best effort.

Our psychology exhibition was an exciting but challenging event, filled with struggles within our group.

My boy had it especially hard—he travelled almost five hours daily while juggling the department function and the exhibition work. It was a crucial time, yet he was being pushed aside. One senior, a friend, and a guide made him feel like his contributions were minimal. Their words affected him so much that he decided to step back and drop out of the group entirely.

I couldn'tcouldn't let that happen. He had worked so hard, and because others failed to acknowledge it, I wouldn't allow him to feel like he didn't belong. I consoled him, assured him his presence was valuable, and convinced him to return, ignoring what others had to say.

But this wasn't the only hurdle. One of my friends in the group got angry at me for taking the lead in deciding what should be done for the exhibition. I didn't understand her reaction—was it jealousy? Frustration? Or something else entirely?

Whatever it was, she shouted at me, making me question my position in the group.

But despite the tensions, I was determined: I wouldn't let these issues break the spirit of our work, especially not for him.

Through all this, I saw how much he cared about the exhibition and doing things correctly. And I cared, too. That's why I fought for him to stay.

Even if he never knew how much it mattered to me, we worked tirelessly, pouring our hearts and souls into the exhibition despite the limited time and resources.

We wanted to win first prize. It wasn't just about competing; it was about proving that our efforts and determination, despite many restrictions and no guidance from the department, were enough to prove ourselves.

But fate had other plans.

When the results were announced, we were shocked; we felt that something unfair had happened to us. Even though we put in all our hard work, we were not awarded any prize.

The reason given was absurd, something that felt unfair and unjustified. The disappointment hit terribly, and I couldn't help.

After everything we had endured—the sacrifices, the sleepless hours, even under the least help from the department side—it felt devastating to walk away empty-handed.

I couldn'tcouldn't hold back my emotions any longer. Tears welled up in my eyes, and before I knew it, I was breaking down. Overwhelmed and unable to process my feelings, I instinctively ran to him. He was there, calm yet equally disappointed, struggling to accept our loss. Without hesitation, I sat beside him, buried my face in his lap, and let the tears flow.

For the first time, I allowed myself to cry openly in front of him—not out of anger or frustration, but sheer sadness.

I can't control myself; my tears soaked his pants, my running nose making it embarrassing. But he didn't give up.

He didn't leave me alone, give me advice, or make me uncomfortable. Instead, he sat for me there, listening to me, and patted my head softly in silence, letting me grieve the moment and wait until I got some relaxation.

In that instant, I realized something profound. It wasn't about winning or losing anymore.

It was about the comfort of having someone who wouldn't judge me, share my pain and accept me at my most vulnerable. He was my safe space. I lost a competition that day, but I gained something far more valuable—the feeling of being truly understood.

1.14: A Celebration to Remember

He had a genuine passion for celebrating birthdays, so he always made those around him feel valued and cherished on their special days. Recognizing this, our group of friends, including around 7 to 12 members and one of our seniors, set out to make his 19th birthday unforgettable. Wanting my gift to carry deep meaning, I sought helpful items and spread joy and warmth.

After much thought, I carefully planned for gifts:

7 PM flower seeds, as I wanted him to enjoy the fragrance of the flower every day.

A violet-colored pen, as I recently got to know about his fondness for that particular color.

A portrait of him, drawn by me, to give a personal touch

Four carefully chosen books—a mix of self-help and a romance novel, meant to inspire his personal growth and warm his heart with tales of love.

- A pre-birthday gift of Freud's The Interpretation of Dreams, a book that took me months to procure.

I also made a mental note to keep track of his reading interests for future gifts.

While my friends contributed their gifts, I was so focused on perfecting my presentation that I hardly noticed theirs.

We decided to celebrate his birthday at college, his favorite environment filled with familiar faces. But the question arose: where exactly should we host it? Remembering our staff hod's faces, we couldn't find a place in classrooms, the exam halls (E and NH) felt too impersonal, and our department was locked, much to our chagrin. Then, inspiration struck like lightning—I recalled the newly established counseling room, a bright, inviting space we had meticulously cleaned and organized together. It was an ideal place for the surprise. After blindfolding him, we led him through the corridors, and he had no idea where we were taking him.

For the cake, I chose a lavish purple ice cream cake, his favorite color—a delightful fusion of sweetness and vibrancy. Transporting it from the bakery while ensuring it didn't melt was quite the challenge, and my palms felt like they had turned to ice from the chilling pressure of holding the box.

One of our friends accompanied us, and we rushed from the Presidency to Akshaya Bakery, hoping to keep the cake intact.

Adorned with the words "We Love You" elegantly scrawled on top, it was a subtle yet poignant declaration of our affection that I was too shy to express directly.

Upon our arrival at the college campus, we positioned him at the center with colossal excitement; we surrounded him, playfully 'proposed' to him, and showed our friendly love for him to make the moment light-hearted and warm.

Later that afternoon, I made him prepare an omelet in the college canteen. I wanted him to attempt something new and adventurous.

Alas, my plans were defeated; by the time the dish was ready, it had vanished before I could snag even a tiny taste, devoured by our eager friends.

The day concluded beautifully, filled with laughter and fun; after classes, my other friends took him to PWD for a meal, while I, as a hosteller, had to bow out at 5:30 pm5:30 PM. Still, my heart filled with contentment, knowing I had played a part in making him happy.

His 19th birthday became the most happening celebration I had planned for him.

As life swept us into a pool of studies, emotions, and personal trials, I found replicating such grand celebrations in subsequent years challenging. However, I resolutely promised myself that in the future, I would do everything in my power to ensure he felt even more cherished and joyous on his birthdays than ever before.

1.15: A Conversation That brightened My Day

As days passed, I spent more time with him—throughout the day in college and even at night, engaged in endless discussions.

We spoke about everything under the sky—books, music, movies, politics- and there was never a topic too big or too small. Our conversations felt limitless, a world of thoughts and interests exchanged between just the two of us.

One day, I was reading the book "pennin marupakkam" by psychiatrist Dr. Shalini.

It offered profound insights into unfamiliar aspects of women's experiences, including their sexuality, emotions, and the struggles they face. As I read, my mind buzzed with thoughts, and I felt an intense urge to share them with someone. I called him.

We started with essential discussions, but soon, I delved deep into the topics of menstruation, menopause, and the psychological, emotional, and sexual changes women experience. As I spoke, he listened intently, absorbing every word. What admired me was his curiosity—not out of mere interest but genuine concern. He asked questions about periods, the usage of sanitary napkins, and the challenges women go through. His attentiveness made me even more enthusiastic to share, and I explained everything with energy and passion.

At one point, I paused and casually asked, "Have you ever bought napkins for your girlfriend?" I knew through some friends (as mentioned in Chapter 7) that he might have had one.

Without hesitation, he laughed and said, "I never had a girlfriend. But I did have a crush on a girl with beautiful eyes back in 10th grade. It was unexpressed, though."

When those words left his mouth, I felt like I had been lifted from the ground into the sky. I was beyond happy. Three things made my heart leap:

I had heard directly from him that he never had a girlfriend.

His so-called 'crush' was nothing more than an unspoken admiration from years ago.

In the simplest of words, he was single.

That single revelation made my entire day. I was at peace—ultimately, utterly peaceful. Knowing he was single felt like the best news I could have received.

And just like that, my heart felt lighter than ever before.

1.16: Carrying the Weight of Final Year

I completed 15 chapters, right? So far, He has been my constant—my safe place. I always found my way to him, whether happiness or sadness, excitement or disappointment. He was the one who listened to me, shared my joy, and held me through my lows. Whenever I felt overwhelmed, he was there, grounding me. But did our relationship continue to flow this smoothly forever? Let's see...

As we stepped into our final year, life changed drastically. Gone were the language classes, and now we had five-hour-long department classes, practical sessions, and a fully packed schedule. Our days were more structured and more demanding. We had HR and Organizational Behavior as our first-hour subjects, and missing attendance was not an option. We rushed to class every morning, making sure not to be even a second late.

Beyond the academic pressure, another fear quietly crept into my mind—What next? Being in my final year meant thinking about postgraduate studies. I am a hostelite and someone who didn't belong to Chennai; my future felt uncertain.

My parents, always eager to provide the best for me, expected me to pursue my PG at a prestigious institute, maybe even abroad.

They would do anything to ensure I got the finest education.

But the thought of leaving...leaving the Presidency, my professors who had become like family, and most of all, him—was unbearable.

How could I imagine my days without our conversations, without his presence in my daily routine?

The thought of being away from him felt heavier than any academic challenge.

So what was I supposed to do now? Should I follow my parents' expectations and risk the distance, or should I fight to stay closer to the life I had built here? The dilemma consumed me, and I wasn't sure if I was ready to face what lay ahead...

1.17: The trials of Final Year

Final year... I wanted to complete it with a good percentage. Rather than wasting time, I tried to make it effective by thoroughly learning all my subjects, especially research methodology, which was very important for higher studies.

I didn't want to struggle later, so I was determined to utilize my time well and learn from my professors, who I knew would help.

We had practicals—psychology practicals. We have never really experienced them in depth for the past two years. We were paired up as subject and experimenter throughout the semester to complete the experiments efficiently and without delay. I wanted to pair up with him, but what do I do? Another girl had already asked him; being generous, he didn't say no. Fine. I sat with another girl, a hardworking and determined friend. Together, we completed most of our experiments quickly. On his side, however, delays occurred due to his partner, so I ended up helping him complete his work later. If only he had chosen me in the first place... I thought.

He was good at all assessments. I still remember struggling to finish the last two levels of the Tower of Hanoi and other experiments.

With only three months left in our undergraduate journey, we learned about paper presentations and research opportunities. My curiosity spiked, and I asked him and two of my close friends if they wanted to conduct research as a final-year achievement. They agreed.

We approached our professor with our idea, and to our delight, she accepted and encouraged us.

She introduced us to an institution in Dindigul for presenting our research work. We started preparing With great enthusiasm, even though we had little knowledge about research. Our professor guided us step by step despite her busy schedule.

Fortunately, I was paired up with him while the other two formed another team. We took our project seriously. We even created a 75-question survey related to our study. But later, we realized that psychological research requires standardized questionnaires or a lengthy standardization process if we create our own. Time was against us. We had only weeks. Our professor advised us to search for a standardized questionnaire, but our theme was so unique that finding a relevant one was difficult.

This led to many moments of frustration, burnout, and doubt. I had several breakdowns, and he, as always, bore the brunt of my frustration. Step by step, however, we managed to find a suitable questionnaire and proceeded with the research. It was a now-or-never situation.

Determinedly, we completed the abstract and consulted our professor despite her hectic schedule. She taught us how to use SPSS, and we managed to analyze our data. Our only goal was to complete it successfully. And we did! We presented our paper. It wasn't perfect, but for our first presentation, we gave our best.

Soon after, another opportunity came at Madras University, where we were guided by one of our senior professors—a person we respected and admired but also feared a little. This time, we performed even better. We eventually succeeded, and our research was even published.

The journey of research work and working as a team was a rollercoaster, but in the end, we got closer than before. With every step, I found him beside me in all adversities.

But as our final year neared its end, a new question loomed over me—what happens next???

1.18: The Unspoken Truth

We began to spend more time together, not for departmental obligations or as class representatives involved in various activities, but as final-year psychology students deeply committed to making the most of our academic journey.

As we shared study sessions filled with dreams and spirited discussions about our field, it became apparent to our classmates that we were developing a connection beyond mere friendship.

Even the girls in our close-knit friend circle, who had been interested in him, began to feel a growing sense of unease and discomfort at the sight of my frequent company.

I wanted to be friendly with them. Iand I tried to be inclusive by sharing joyful moments and having fun together, and I had a good time with them.

However, I soon sensed a shift in their approach. Even as a part of a group, I later realized I was never entirely accepted as one of them.

My presence was met with hesitation and irritation.

Later, I realized they felt uncomfortable during my time with him.

Was their behavior driven by jealousy, possessiveness, or just human nature?

They even believed I had distanced him from them. But was I wrong to prioritize what we wanted for our future? Was it selfish to focus on something meaningful?

Even during our research paperwork, we both had a big fight because of those same friends—the girls who were closer to him and didn't want me to be with him. They made a big mess by deliberately stopping him from coming with me to work on our paper, which had to be submitted to the university that evening via email. It was the last-minute rush to check the final version and send it in, and I needed his presence to complete the work as a co-author.

But those girls intentionally dragged the time until 3:30 PM at college, even knowing we had to submit the paper by 5 PM sharp.

This made me very much furious. I asked him to come with me to finish the work, but they wouldn't let him go. Unable to bear it, I walked towards the university alone, crying and feeling emotionally broken.

My mind was racing with frustration. Wasn't this important to him? How could he not see what they were doing? My anger wasn't just towards him but also towards those girls who seemed to enjoy seeing me in pain.

When I reached the university, I sat where we used to work and broke down, crying loudly since no one was around. I tried calling my friend from the hostel, but she didn't pick up. I was suffocating, overwhelmed, and even hunger gnawed at me, but I had lost all motivation to continue.

After 30–40 minutes, he finally arrived, having spoken to them before coming. My anger had only developed then, and I was at my peak. He silently sat beside me and opened a lunch box. I knew he hadn't eaten either. Taking a spoon, he gently tried to feed me. But my emotions had shot up.

In my anger, I shouted,

"Even if my mom was in your place, I wouldn't let her feed me."

It wasn't just about the food; everything that had piled inside me. I knew the words cut deep.

I can feel it through his eyes.

He was hurt, broken even. (I am sorry, Varun)

But I couldn't stop myself. I was drowning in frustration, unable to balance my emotions.

Despite everything, we completed our research paper and successfully published it. Did we sort out the problem between us? The paper was done, but something still felt unresolved. Were we moving forward without addressing what had happened? Was this just a temporary silence before another storm?

Then came that day—one of the worst I had faced.

They called us and interrogated us. "Are you both dating?" "What's going on between you two?"

I was cornered, but hearing his response shook me the most.

"No, she's my friend."

There it was—my answer.

A simple line, but I didn't know what to say.

When they turned to me next, I had no choice but to mirror his words. "No, we are just friends. Nothing more."

I said it with a straight face, but inside, I felt something shatter.

It wasn't the right time to reveal the truth; what if it made things worse?

Even so, I couldn't bring myself to leave. I didn't want to.

What if he needed me? What if, one day, he searched for me, and I was gone? Could I walk away without a reason?

And then, another fear took hold of me—what comes next?

Would we still be together after graduation, or were we just two months away from going our separate ways?

Only time will tell...

1.19: Embracing the Uncertain Goodbye

Final year's final days approached.

We were busy with our semester practicals, knowing we would finish our undergraduate journey in less than a week.

I happily prepared for practicals with him, wanting to cherish those last memorable moments. He believes that no matter what the future brings, let's be happy. We sat together, studying every experiment and assessment, determined to make our practicals the best they could be—without realizing what would happen the next day.

The night before our assessment practicals (as we had already completed our experiment practicals), we received the news about COVID-19. Exams might get postponed.

At first, I felt a strange happiness, a slight relief about the postponement of exams, but soon the seriousness of the situation hit.

Hostel students were asked to return home immediately as the virus worsened.

It was an uncertain and terrifying time, not just for the world but for us. The fear of separation ruled over me. I couldn't express my feelings—I knew we were just good friends, but if I told him now, wouldn't it become the worst goodbye ever?

I knew I would miss him, but I couldn't say it. I forgot everything—his eyes, his face, his voice, his scent, his sweat, his silence, his calmness, his touch, his presence became my everything. And at last, I didn't want to miss him. My heart and soul searched for him, longing for his presence, but I had no choice. I returned home with no idea what the future held.

Weeks later, we were informed that our practicals would be conducted online, like a viva. Our final semester was later performed as an open-book test. We kept in touch, but I missed him more than ever. We finished our undergraduate degree, but everything felt incomplete.

Slowly, we started talking more through WhatsApp, Telegram, and even occasional phone calls. I spent hours away from my family to speak to him upstairs. Long distance was hard.

We began sharing more movies, books, and thoughts. He watched a lot of series and shared them with me.

I searched and picked PDFs of books, and we both had a mutual interest in Durjoy Datta's novels.

Days passed, and the time for our PG admissions arrived. The next chapter of our lives was about to begin. Looking back,

The moments that once felt insignificant now reveal a deeper meaning, like puzzle pieces coming together.

This was just the beginning. Little did I know that the journey ahead would bring unexpected encounters, emotions beyond my understanding, and a connection that would transform my understanding of love.

And so, the story unfolds...

2
New Beginning

2.1: Amidst Uncertainty

As our final year approached its end, life took an unexpected turn.

The world was stunned by the arrival of COVID-19, and so did our carefully laid-out plans. What was supposed to be a memorable last semester filled with final moments in college, celebrations, and goodbyes suddenly became a series of online classes and virtual exams.

Our practical exams were conducted as an online viva session, and our final semester turned into an online, open-book test, something we never imagined would be the conclusion of our undergraduate journey.

We had spent years working hard, navigating emotions, experiences, and friendships, only for our final chapter to feel incomplete.

There was no official farewell, not even online, no one last time classroom chitchats, no walking through those familiar corridors one previous time.

Instead, there were just screens, emails, and the silent realization that an essential phase of our lives had ended without the expected closure.

Through all this, we stayed connected. Our conversations continued over WhatsApp, Telegram, and phone calls. I spent more time on the terrace, away from my family, to talk to him. Long-distance was difficult, and while our bond grew through shared thoughts, books, and series, the uncertainty of the future loomed over us.

As the time for postgraduate admissions arrived, a new wave of worries surfaced. Where would we go next? Would we end up in the same city or drift apart?

The thought of stepping into the next stage of life without him beside me felt unacceptable.

But life had its plans, and we were about to embark on a journey that neither of us expected..

2.2: The in-Between days

Days passed, and the conversations about postgraduate admissions began.

Within a few months, we started applying to colleges, mostly government institutions. We had a plan—to explore new opportunities beyond the Presidency. With our excellent undergraduate percentages, we eagerly applied to various reputed colleges in different districts, excited about the possibilities ahead.

But beneath that excitement, a quiet fear grew inside me. What if we chose different colleges? What if we got separated in the name of education? Though we applied to the same colleges—including the Presidency—uncertainty loomed over me. Would fate keep us together or lead us onto different paths?

Everything had an ending, and change was inevitable. Then, one fine evening, I received a call from one of my professors about the admissions at Presidency. She asked me to come for the admission process. A wave of happiness rushed over me, but along with it came a lingering concern—financial stability during those uncertain COVID times.

I made my decision—I would stay at Presidency. It felt like the right choice, a familiar place that had shaped so much of who I had become. But one question remained unanswered: What if he chose somewhere else?

2.3: The Choice That Mattered

He was more eager to explore colleges beyond the Presidency than me. While the Presidency was one of his preferences, it wasn't as deeply rooted in his heart as in mine. We both received interview calls from RGNIYD, scheduled just a day after the Presidency admission. Oh, and I forgot to mention—he, too, got the call from the Presidency for admission.

He considered coming for admission to the Presidency but also wanted to attempt the RGNIYD interview before making his final decision.

He believed in weighing the pros and cons of choosing based on opportunities and exposure.

Honestly, I couldn't deny that RGNIYD had its charm—it promised growth, a broader horizon, and something new. We both liked it, especially for its library (we both enjoy going to libraries)

We completed our admission process at Presidency, yet my heart refused to rest. A lingering fear clung to me—Would he stay? Would he continue with me, or would he choose a different path?

Then, after almost a year of being apart, I finally saw him in person.

I stood near him, taking in the moment, letting reality sink in. No more phone calls or voices carried through satellites—he was right there before my eyes. And? I was overwhelmed.

My eyes devoured every inch of him. His hair had changed, his face had matured, and even his slight belly—courtesy of lockdown—made me smile. He was no longer the teenage boy I once knew. He was becoming a man. My man.

But just as excitement filled my heart, fear lurked in its corners. What if he chose RGNIYD after clearing the interview?

Would this reunion be just a fleeting moment before another separation?

2.4: The choice that matters

The day after securing our admission to the Presidency, we both attended the interview for RGNIYD. Surprisingly, a familiar face was among the panellists—our own HOD.

The moment I saw her on the screen, panic set in. My palms turned sweaty, my heart pounded, and I could almost hear the unspoken words in her mind: Yesterday, you joined the Presidency. Then why are you here? Her expression said it all.

Unsurprisingly, I failed.

It felt almost deliberate—she ensured we stayed in the Presidency for our postgraduate studies. But somehow, fate had a strange way of making her presence felt wherever I went. If not in person, then through someone else's words. As a senior professor in the field of psychology, she was always there—watching, influencing, and deciding.

Next, it was his turn to enter the Zoom room. Before he went in, I quickly informed him about our HOD's presence.

But not like me; he was calm, confident, and composed. As expected, he cracked the interview effortlessly and secured admission at RGNIYD.

Now, he had two choices—Presidency or RGNIYD.

I was genuinely happy for him, proud of how easily he had cleared the interview. But at the same time, an ache settled deep in my heart. What if he chose RGNIYD? What if I had to continue without him? The thought of missing him, of not seeing him every day, was unbearable.

I asked him what he planned to do. He said I needed a couple of days to decide.

Those two days felt like an eternity. Anxiety consumed me, fear crept into my thoughts, and I couldn't shake off the possibility of losing him to another institution.

Then, finally, his decision came. And it was the one I had been hoping for all along.

He chose the Presidency.

He may have had reasons for picking it, but to me, it meant something else entirely—two more years with him. And that was all I needed to be happy.

2.5: More Than Mere Classmates

So, we were classmates again—but this time, it was different.

It wasn't just about sitting in the same classroom as classmates.

But now, we were best friends, bound by something much more profound than before.

We had become each other's constant, sharing everything under the sky—our thoughts, struggles, laughter, and even the most minor details of our daily lives.

Online classes had no structure, accurate schedule, and no attendance for a namesake; teachers probably felt more stressed. Some days, we would wake up just minutes before class, groggily grabbing our phones or laptops. Attending virtual lectures felt nothing like a real college.

We missed the campus, the rush to class, the hurried last-minute revisions, friendly in-person talks with our professors and most of all—the feeling of actually being there together.

Every morning, we would call each other as soon as class started, making sure neither of us missed it. We weren't just attending classes together—we were surviving them together. Whenever someone else from our batch needed a wake-up call, we also pulled them into the chaos.

But no matter how much we tried to adjust, one truth remained—we missed college life.

We missed the hallways, the random conversations, the energy of the classroom, and the simple joy of seeing each other in person. The screen between us felt like a barrier, but even through it, our bond only grew stronger.

Even if the world had forced us apart, we somehow found a way to be together.

Chapter 2.6: The Confession

Once in a while, our HOD would assign us tasks that made us feel more like real postgraduate students rather than just students doing PG for namesake.

One such task was conducting an online seminar for school students.

He, I, and another friend were responsible for preparing a trainer manual on self-esteem—a project that became one of the most memorable experiences of our virtual academic life.

We spent many hours discussing ideas, exploring new research, and diving into our field.

Late nights blurred into early mornings as we worked together, sharing documents, bouncing ideas off each other, and keeping each other motivated.

And amidst all this, we found small joys.

We started listening to music together while working—sometimes discussing the lyrics, sometimes just letting the melodies fill the silence between our chats. Those moments, though simple, felt like our own little world within the virtual space.

But then, a new challenge arrived—one that tested my patience.

Our HOD asked me to create an invitation for the seminar. Excited, I poured my creativity into it. But the cycle that followed was endless—I made, she corrected. I recreated it, and she corrected it again.

This went on for two days straight.

At first, I was determined to get it well. But as the corrections kept coming, frustration built up inside me.

It felt like I was following orders rather than creating something meaningful and new and listening to my thoughts.

I shared my frustration with him, expecting motivation to do the work or encouragement.

Instead, he said:

"Don't waste your energy on this. Prioritize your own work. Do what matters to you." (actually, none of the others, even my parents, said this to me)

His words hit me harder than I expected.

Was I working just for the sake of it? Was this effort making me happy, or was it just draining me?

But beyond that... his concern for me, his words, his presence—even from miles away—meant more than anything else.

Dear readers, I am asking if you will miss the person who cares for you more than you care for your self.

And in that moment, something inside me shifted.

I didn't need to overthink it. I already knew.

That night, without waiting for the perfect time or caring about whether he would accept it, I typed three words in Telegram.

"I love you."

And then, I slept.

No overthinking. No expectations. No fear.

I had confessed my love.

What happens next? Let's see in the next chapter...

Chapter 2.7: Unreturned love

The very next day, my heart raced.

I had finally confessed my feelings years ago, and now, I only want to hear his response. Deep down, I believed—or maybe I just hoped—that he had feelings for me too.

The way we shared every little thing, the way he cared, the way he was always there... it had to mean something.

I picked up my phone, my hands slightly trembling and called him.

"Did you see my message?" I asked, my voice laced with fear and nervousness.

"Yes."

A pause.

I took a deep breath.

"I meant it," I admitted.

"It wasn't a prank. It wasn't something I said impulsively. I love you, actually not just now, but for years and I want to know—what do you think about this?"

Silence. A heavy, suffocating silence.

Then, finally, he spoke.

"I... don't feel that way about you."

His words hit me like a storm.

"I care for you, but only as a friend. I never had any romantic feelings for you."

The ground beneath me felt like it was slipping away.

No.

This wasn't how it was supposed to go. This wasn't the response I had imagined, the one I had believed in.

My breath hitched. Tears welled up in my eyes, and before I knew it, I was crying—at him, in front of him, because of him.

It felt like a failure. Like I had lost something before it even had the chance to begin. Did I misinterpret everything? Did I overthink every moment we shared?

I wanted to run. To stop talking to him. To erase everything and move on.

But my love for him... refused to let me go.

Sobbing, I whispered, "I don't know if I can do this. I don't know if I can stay."

His voice was calm yet firm.

"If you think this will hurt you in the future, let's stop being together."

That sentence shattered me more than his rejection. Stop being together? How could I do that?

I couldn't imagine a single day without him.

I couldn't imagine not seeing his name on my phone, not hearing his voice, not having him beside me even if he wasn't the person I wanted him to be.

And so, I surrendered.

"Okay," I whispered.

"I won't bring it up again. I wont disturb you based on this. I won't expect anything. Let's just stay like before—just friends."

I apologised if I hurt him. To me, loving is beautiful. Being in love is great, but it should happen by itself.

But deep inside, I knew nothing would ever be the same again.

Chapter 2.8: Love, Unspoken Yet Unyielding

Nothing changed.

Even after his rejection and hearing the words that should have ended everything, my love for him grew deeper, stronger, and more unwavering.

I didn't stop loving him just because he didn't love me back. Love isn't a transaction where you give and expect something in return. It's a feeling that settled into my heart long ago, refusing to fade, no matter how much reality tried to shake it.

I continued silently loving him, just like before my confession. The only difference? I carried the truth that he didn't see me that way. And yet, I stayed.

There were moments when doubt crept in. Should I have walked away? Would staying after rejection make me look desperate?

Am I hurting myself more by holding on? But love doesn't follow logic. My heart chose him, even though he told me to move on.

At times, fear took over. What if my parents found out? What if his parents did? Would they separate us, even as friends?

Did they think of me as a bad girl? Did they think badly about my parenting?

But the strangest part of it all? Nobody knew that I loved him.

Maybe some had suspicions—how my face would involuntarily blush when someone mentioned his name, and my reactions to anything related to him were too obvious. A few of my classmates, seniors, and even professors all saw something between us.

They liked our bond. Some even believed we were a couple.

But what could I do? The one person who truly mattered in this equation felt nothing for me.

And still, no one is to blame. Not him, not me, not fate.

This is how love works most of the time.

It's not always mutual. It doesn't always go the way we dream. Sometimes, we love in silence, with no expectations, no demands—just a quiet, persistent feeling that refuses to let go.

And so, I continued. Loving him, knowing he would never love me back.

This time, I loved him more than ever before.

Chapter 2.9: The Final Year and Our Unbreakable Bond

Finally, we were in the final year of our postgraduate journey.

Unlike our undergraduate days, when classrooms were crowded with students, our PG batch was small—just 18 of us. And even among those 18, some rarely came to college, while others belonged to a different division.

It was just us.

After many discussions, debates, and second thoughts, we chose School Psychology as our specialization. It wasn't an easy decision, but somehow, we ended up walking the same path again—this time under the guidance of our HOD.

We learned together, explored new ideas, and figured things out ourselves. Online exams became part of our routine, and like most students during that time, we shared notes, copied answers, and survived through teamwork. It was no secret—everyone did it. But what made it special was that we did it together.

Then, as the world slowly opened up, our lives returned to normal.

Classes resumed offline, and suddenly, we were back in the familiar halls of our college. The screens between us were gone.

We went to college together. We spent time together. We laughed, fought over silly things, worked on assignments, and prepared for exams—just like always.

But after lockdown, exams felt like a real task again. The ease of online tests was gone; now, we had to focus truly. Yet, nothing felt too tricky because we had each other.

And just like that, 1.5 years of our postgraduation flew by.

The days passed, but one thing remained unchanged—us.

Chapter 2.10: Love in Silence, Unity in Action

My love for him never changed. If anything, it only grew deeper.

But I became more conscious than ever about not showing it—not to him or anyone. It wasn't about hiding my feelings; it was about protecting both of us from the pain that would follow.

Being friends and becoming lovers is a beautiful journey, but when love is one-sided, it becomes silent suffering.

So, I kept my love inside me, held it in my heart without expectations, without forcing it on him.

Even if it was heavy, I felt he deserved to be loved more.

We were in our final year, our final semester, standing at the edge of another ending. But before that, we had one last challenge ahead:

Our dissertation

Block placement

Case study collection

All are happening simultaneously.

These weren't just minor tasks but necessities of our degree.

And yet, amidst all the stress and deadlines, I enjoyed every second of it.

Because I was with him. Day and night.

We worked tirelessly—helping each other, brainstorming ideas, pushing through sleepless nights. We never worked without each other. His project, my project—it never felt separate. We tackled everything together.

I loved being beside him, watching him think, discuss, and create. Even in the chaos, I found happiness—because he was there.

And when the final day arrived—the day we submitted our hard work—the sense of joy and satisfaction was unforgettable.

But the most precious moments?

They weren't just in the work.

In collecting case studies, we created some of our most beautiful memories.

And those? I'll tell you in the next chapter...

Chapter 2.11: A Journey Through Our Past and Present

As we neared the completion of our final-year work, one of the most memorable experiences was collecting case studies. It wasn't just an academic requirement but a journey through our past and present.

The first stop? His school.

He brought me to where his childhood had unfolded, the classrooms where he once sat as a little boy with a runny nose and teary eyes, missing his mother.

He was so excited to be back, to walk through the pathway of his past, and to relive his memories with me beside him. he speaks, and I listen; I always love the spark in his eyes while he talks about his childhood.

I stood there, listening to his stories—the teachers he adored, the mischief he got into, the lessons he learned.

It felt nostalgic, watching him reconnect with the world that made him.

We met his school principal, who welcomed us warmly and permitted us to conduct our case studies.

Working with the children was an adorable experience, but the most memorable part was knowing that this was where his journey had begun.

But another unforgettable moment awaited.

Next, I brought him into my world.

I took him to my hometown—the school my mother had been running for nearly three decades. This time, we weren't alone. Two of my beloved juniors joined us on this journey, making the experience even more special.

The journey was long—seven hours away—but every second was worth it because he was with me.

Seeing him at my home, in my room, walking across my terrace was a feeling I couldn't describe.

"Who wouldn't love seeing the person they cherish blend into their world?"

Despite my parents' suspicions (because, of course, Indian parents), I somehow made it happen. I brought him into my world, just as he had brought me into his.

And together, we completed our final-year case study—our last big project as postgraduate students.

A New Beginning Awaits...

Dear readers, thank you for walking through this journey with me.

But this isn't the end.

The story continues—our story continues. But I believe this book should end here. Because what comes next? That's another book, another journey, another chapter of life.

Please support my writing as I begin again.

And if you have any thoughts, feelings, or feedback—I would love to hear them.

Until next time... ?

Further Reading/more From The Author

Varnaa is working on Part 2 of To Me, He is Love, exploring life after college—the journey through jobs, career challenges, and the personal and professional struggles that shaped her path.

Varnaa is a budding writer, blogger, and poet who brings raw emotions to life through her words. Passionate about real-life experiences, she strives to connect with readers by capturing love, longing, and unspoken feelings.

If To Me, He is Love touched your heart, I would love to hear your thoughts!

? Leave a review – Your words mean the world and help this story reach more hearts.

? Follow me on

- Instagram @bookipookies
- Pinterest @bookipookies
- YouTube @bookipookies
- Website - www.bookipookies.com

for exclusive book updates, poetry, and behind-the-scenes content. For more books from the author check out www.bookiepookies.com

? Stay connected – Be the first to know about my next book by joining my blog and newsletter.

Your support keeps this journey alive! Let's celebrate love, emotions, and storytelling together. ♥?

www.ingramcontent.com/pod-product-compliance
Lightning Source LLC
Chambersburg PA
CBHW020458160726
47991CB00007B/2717